BY LJ ALONGE

Grosset & Dunlap
An Imprint of Penguin Random House

CHAPTER 1

ALL-AMERICAN BEEF

When Frank's raging like he is right now, you just have to let him get it out of his system. If you tell him to cool it, you'll only make things worse. We're walking down Telegraph, and every time we stop at a corner, he tries to knock over a trash can. They're the old steel ones that sound like a car wreck when they hit the sidewalk. Frank's still waiting on his growth spurt; he needs a running start and hard kick to get the cans over. The one he knocks over now rolls halfway into the street, emptying its Styrofoam guts in the bike lane before settling in the gutter.

"Nice one," I say, hoping it's the last.

"Shut up," he says. "You ain't helping."

"Trash can didn't do nothing to me."

He wipes his hands, the way people do when they're proud of their work.

"Feel better?" I ask.

"Like a champ," he says.

The problem is money. We have none, we never have any, but today's the last straw. We've been to a pizza place and a wing place and a sub place. They looked at both of my wrinkled dollars like they were covered in slime and pointed their snooty fingers over our heads, to the door. We left as Frank insulted their food, his stomach growling noisily the whole time. We just tried to eat and run at this Korean place, but they threw us out after the salads. I've still got the taste of ranch dressing stuck in my mouth.

"You know what I'm gonna do with my first million?" Frank says, trying to work another can into the street.

"Invest in the stock market."

"No. That's some nerdy shit *you* would do. You'd probably throw it all away on books. No—what *I* would do is buy a restaurant. That way, I could have them deliver food to my house for free every day. Grilled cheese every day. Free."

A million dollars and he'd eat grilled cheese every day. That's Frank in a nutshell.

"Sounds good," I tell him. "But what are we doing in the meantime?"

He sighs. "Don't know."

After some thought I say, "I'd probably build a couple schools," thinking it's the right thing to say, but by then Frank's lost interest. So we're standing on the corner, sulking, when a group of kids walks past us, laughing, pushing, their hands stuffed into the bottom of a greasy paper bag.

"Where'd y'all get that?" Frank asks.

"Up the street," one of the kids says. There's a mush of fries in the back of his mouth. "Want some?"

My mom says nobody but con artists and churchfolk give you things for no reason. This kid looks tricky. He's a heavyweight whose lips shine with grease. Just watching him chew makes me uneasy.

"Yeah," Frank says, reaching out his

hand. "Lemme grab a couple."

"No problem," the kid says, pouring the fries onto the sidewalk. "Eat up."

A soggy knot of fries goes spilling out between us. A dark puddle of oil forms around the edges. It's not that funny, but the kids are laughing so hard, they keep falling over each other.

"Eat!" Grease Lips repeats.

Instead, Frank steps on the pile. Potato mush covers his shoes. He's got his jaw clenched and his fists balled up. The guys keep laughing. Frank's not afraid of a fight, but with his size, it's hard to take him seriously. Plus there's six of them. They keep talking. They can't believe we fell for it. They want to know if we enjoy being such huge pussies. They're gasping for air.

I'm six feet four inches, but you can tell right away I'm no fighter. I breathe a secret sigh of relief when Frank eventually turns and stomps off.

"I woulda fought them," Frank says. Now he's kicking random things—a fire hydrant, a newspaper stand, bikes. "But I got probation."

"I know," I say.

"Remember when I used to carry a pocket knife?"

"Yup."

He makes a couple of showy stabbing motions. "It had a switch so you could just flip it open fast." The truth is, Frank's never seriously hurt anyone. He just really likes to hear himself talk.

I slow down as we pass Benny's Taco

Truck, this being one of the few times there's no line. Frank says he knows people who've worked there, and from the stories they tell, it's a one-way ticket to the ER. It's a terrible day to be out wandering—it must be a thousand degrees out. Even the dealers and junkies are sticking to the shade, but here we are, about to be burned alive on a two-dollar lunch mission. I'm feeling dizzy, so I say we should stop in the donut shop, the one with air-conditioning.

"Sure," Frank says, rolling his eyes, "maybe they'll sell us some bread crusts."

By the time we pass McDonald's, I've had it. Two bucks there goes about as far as it'll get you anywhere. I start walking between the cars in the parking lot, careful not to touch their burning doors.

"Gross," Frank says, but then he remembers the money's in my pocket and follows.

Inside, I close my eyes and wait for the air-conditioning to close in around me. I lift my shirt up a little so the air hits my stomach. To my surprise, it's warm. There must be forty, fifty people in here, whole families crowded into a single booth. Ms. Mayfair has her wheelchair stationed right over an air vent. Mr. Chalmers is sitting near the window, playing chess with his buddies, all of them stripped down to tank tops, fanning themselves with old newspapers. Little Chucky Jackson is going from table to table, doing a little jig as he asks for ice.

In a booth in the far corner is Pop.

"Shit," I say.

When I was a kid, when he was still living with us, people used to say we looked alike: same skinny face and high cheekbones and bug eyes. Same dark skin. Even now I know the resemblance is still there. When people look at us, they can tell he's my dad. But right now he's looking worse than ever. He's in a dirty wifebeater and these ratty black jeans that he obviously skimmed off a much bigger guy. Bits of twig are stuck in his Afro. When he runs his hand through his hair, it just stays in place like it's glued in. It's almost a miracle that I don't die of embarrassment on the spot.

"We gotta leave," I tell Frank.

"No can do," Frank says. "Already put in my order."

"Then cancel the freaking order."

"You just can't go around making and canceling orders, Justin." He winks at the cashier, a cutie with tiny beads of sweat above her lip. "It's a bad look. And unclassy."

Frank almost never goes to school, but when he gets around a girl, he starts laying the SAT words on thick. "*Unclassy*? Frank, *unclassy* ain't a word."

"Maybe it is, maybe it ain't. What I do know is that this young lady is waiting for you to acquire some nutrition."

The cashier's giving me a look. Every girl has that look, the one that tells you they'll bite your head off if you say anything remotely smart-ass. One eyebrow cocked up, mouth in a pinch. It always gets me all tight in the chest.

"Chicken sandwich," I say. I pull out my couple of crumpled dollars and carefully smooth them out. "And some waters. But hurry up, please."

She's repeating our order when a kind of grumbling sound starts up behind me. Like someone's clearing his throat.

"Justin," Frank says, looking behind us.

"Don't look," I hiss.

But the throat clearing's getting louder, and now the cashier is giving me the look *again*. Like it's *me* making the sound. What does she want me to do? I've got no control over Pop. Whenever he sees me in public, he goes out of his way to talk to me or challenge me to a game of one-on-one like the old days. And whenever I see him, I hide or walk the other way or pretend I don't hear him calling.

I close my eyes and wait a few seconds to see if he'll get the hint that I don't want to talk to him. But of course he just gets louder. I turn around, and there he is, with a wide, satisfied smile on his face, one hand helping to prop him up against the ketchup dispenser. A hearty stream of ketchup squirts out onto the counter.

"Where I'm from," he says, swaying, "a boy says hello when he sees his father."

"Hi," I say.

"Wassup, Mr. Shaw," Frank says.

"Good," Pop says. "Very good."

Pop's two buddies frown at each other to show how impressed they are with him, the type of man who commands respect from his son. They're winos, like him. A part of me is happy that Pop is at least in better shape than them, with their plaid shorts and combat boots and wild beards. Their teeth like candy corn. They look at us, tipping their imaginary caps.

"He's embarrassed by me," Pop says to them. "That's why he's acting all shy."

"I ain't embarrassed," I say.

"You look it."

"I'm not."

"Then gimme a hug."

He looks shrunken and skinny, like my arms might wrap around him a few times. He opens his arms wide. Hair sprouts thickly from his armpits. Pop sleeps on the streets now. I couldn't tell you exactly where. When Mom kicked him out, she said he'd be staying at a Motel 6 down the street, but I knew better. I used to imagine him foraging behind churches or the Dunkin' Donuts, up to his neck in trash. I'd imagine him waiting outside of drive-thrus, asking people to add a taco or burger to their order. For a while every hobo I saw started to look like him.

"No," I say.

"Too good for a hug?"

"You're drunk," I say.

"I'm a man," Pop says. "I can have a drink whenever and wherever I please, thankyouverymuch."

No one's making a sound, not even loud-ass Frank. It's the heavy kind of silence that comes right before a fight. Everyone's stopped eating, their hands frozen in midair. Even the dude on the frier comes out to watch. I'm wishing I was just about anywhere else in the world, somewhere far away, out in Middle Earth maybe.

"How about a little game of one-on-one?" Pop says. He does a crossover with an imaginary ball. "Like we used to."

"How about you stink!" I say, pushing past him. It's the meanest thing I can think of.

CHAPTER 2

GEORGE AND LENNY 2.0

Frank and I walk down Telegraph, moving slow when we pass under the shade of an awning or tree. Everybody's got their Saturday hustle going. A rusted truck puffs out black smoke as it pulls up on Fifty-Second; three guys in cowboy hats jump out and start arranging big boxes of strawberries at the intersection. There's a young homeless guy out on an island in the middle of the street holding up a NEED MONEY FOR WEED sign. At the gas station, a group of kids are setting up a car wash and laughing; mostly they spray the water on one another and then get mad when someone takes it too far. An old-school Impala—purple and black with orange flames on the side—comes roaring out of the station. I watch it run a red light and pull onto the I-980 on-ramp.

We're on our way to Bushrod—Frank and I go there every day to play ball. I'm no good, a mess of arms and legs, uncoordinated like you wouldn't believe. Everybody knows me as Frank's tall friend, the kid who dribbles the ball off his foot. Frank thinks it's pretty funny, but I'd always pictured this summer as the summer things would change. I grew seven inches in the spring. Now people *notice* me. They take long looks out of the corners of their eyes.

I stand there and pretend not to notice, hoping they stare a little longer. You go your whole life in the shadows, not being noticed by anybody, and all of a sudden it's like you've won *American Idol*. I'd be lying if I told you it didn't feel good.

But at Bushrod I'm a nobody. A zero. No one picks me to play, no one notices when I come or go. What I do is, I sit on the grass and I watch. And I learn: how the coolest kids never raise their voices when they talk. How they always slouch a little to the side, like half their body is heavier than the other. How they spit every couple of minutes and roll their shirtsleeves up just above their tattoos. How they break shit to remind everyone of how bad they are. From the grass I watch and listen, and when I get home at night, I download it all into a black notebook like a spy.

We stop a couple of blocks away from the park and sit down under the shade of an oak tree to eat our food. "How much you want to bet," Frank says, "I can bag the next girl that walks by?" When there's nothing left to talk about, when Frank and I have gotten tired of clowning each other or run out of ways to spend our future millions, we talk about girls. We've laid waste to whole afternoons analyzing the way a girl chews gum. I wonder if these girls know that even the coldest glance, the look you'd give a roach skittering across the kitchen, can send us into orbit.

"You know you're gonna win," I say.

"We ain't started and you giving up?"

"I'm just saying."

Frank starts primping. He's got cool hair that he gels down, action-movie good looks, and some crazy charisma to top it off. It leaves girls hypnotized. They're drawn to him like squirrels to nuts, raccoons to trash. I've seen him Pepe Le Pew his way through whole crews of ladies.

Secretly, I'm hoping for a monster to walk by, a freak show with black nail polish and purple contacts. That'll show him. But the first girl that walks toward us is this goody-goody from school. She's always talking about the recital she was late for or the new instrument she's being forced to play or the college courses she's studying for. Right now she's carrying a stack of books in her arms.

"All yours, buddy," Frank says, pushing me into her.

"Hey!" I say.

"Hey," she says. The leaves throw crooked shadows over our faces. I think she's smiling, but I'm not sure.

"Weird seeing you around!"

"Yeah." She looks down at her books. Each one is dictionary thick. "Just left the library."

"And I'm just standing here! Weird! Like fate, almost. Us seeing each other. Here! On the street!"

The guys at the park tell stories about their girls. All of them have two or three that love them to death. You wonder with all the time they spend at the park how they could possibly keep all the girls happy.

Anyway, there's supposedly a way to talk to girls that drives them crazy—like you don't care about them at all. Then you've got to talk about how good they look, how you wish you could get a taste. I've got pages of notes on this.

"Real hot today!" I say.

"Yup," she says.

"Good thing you're heading home! I bet you're hot!"

"Yup."

"As in temperature! But also beauty, too!"

Behind me I hear Frank slapping his forehead. "Yo," he says, "how would you like to go out with my friend here?"

She laughs, then starts snapping her fingers. "I know you."

"From class," I say. "History."

"Oh," she says. "Yeah, that. I knew you looked familiar."

"My man Justin," Frank jumps in. "He's got a face you can't forget."

"Well, no," she says to me, "I mean, yes, I remember you from class. But it's just that—there's a guy that looks *just* like you outside the Marriott, throwing up in the fountain."

CHAPTER 3
IN WHICH I DO AN ADEQUATE JUDAS IMPRESSION

I forgot to mention: Today's the day I'm supposed to throw a brick through the window at Q Mart. Frank's dragging his feet a little, raking his fingers across the gates as he walks. It's cooler now; there's even a little breeze coming off the bay. People are starting to come out and sit on their stoops and porches, like they're out to cheer me on.

"Come on," I say. "We gotta get there before everyone leaves."

"You're not really gonna do it," he says.

"Yes, I am."

"I thought you were just *saying* you'd do it. For the cool points."

"I guess you'll have to see."

"*I* wouldn't even do it. That should tell you something."

He says this plan is the dumbest thing he's ever heard. He says he'd expect a kid as smart as me to see through it. Why would you want to impress dudes who don't even like you? And why would anyone like you for throwing a brick through a window?

"What if," Frank continues, "you just knock over a couple of the book stands. That sounds more like you."

"That's the problem," I say. "I don't want that to sound like me."

Sometimes, when the guys at the park start busting my balls about things like my virginity, I walk over to the Q Mart and talk to Omar, the Nigerian owner. When he bought the store, he had big plans to rebuild it, but everywhere you look there's a mess of electrical wires or a pool of water from the leaking fridges in the back. Most of his shelves are only half stocked with crap no one wants: anchovies in hot sauce, those tiny watch batteries, paperback romance novels.

"Let them talk!" he said once. He was eating a tin of anchovies; he'd made a "miscalculation of American taste preferences" and now had a storeroom full of them. "I wish I had a son like you! You don't steal! You don't talk back! In Nigeria there would be women banging down your door! You're a good boy!"

"Maybe I don't wanna be a 'good boy,'" I whined.

He stopped chewing. "Why would you want to not be a good boy?"

But how could he understand? It's not that Bushrod's some special place for basketball. It's not Rucker or anything. Usually no one comes to the park except the kids who live close by. The courts are outside this closed-down middle school. The concrete's cracked, with little weeds shooting out of it. The lines are faint, and some of the backboards have been ripped off. Next to us is an overgrown grass field where a lot of older Mexican dudes play soccer. Sometimes white college kids will come down from Berkeley and play Frisbee there, too. Next to that is an abandoned baseball field, where stray dogs have litters in the dugouts.

No doubt there are better courts elsewhere, like the ones down by the lake or the new ones off Bancroft in the east. But there's no park like the one in your neighborhood. Technically I could go to some off-brand park nearby, play a few games with kids I've never met and make some friends. But what's the point of that? You want to be able to walk through your neighborhood with pride, with your head held high. You want to be able to go to the park and have people recognize you, call out your name. Otherwise, you're just a sucker with no place to call your own. You're invisible. And I'm tired of being invisible.

When we get to Bushrod, a few guys are sitting in a circle at half-court. Similac sits in the middle, trying to spin the ball on his finger. When the ball rolls off, one of the kids picks it up and hands it back to him like an offering. He's shirtless; the muscles popping out of his shoulders look like they might break the skin at any moment. On the court he's a terror, more brawler than basketball player. Many kids have walked away from a game with a busted lip or broken nose. It's easy to picture Similac twenty years out, working as a bouncer at some club.

When he sees me, he smiles. He's got small gray teeth that everyone thinks are actually his baby teeth. *Not enough Similac as a baby*, they whisper. His lip comes to rest in a relaxed snarl.

"Our hero returns," he says. "Hey, *Justin*."

Everyone gets a nickname around here: Similac, Fat Jimmy, Clorox, Bo Jenkins, Shimmy, and Stooge. Me? They just call me *Justin*—with that little bit of extra emphasis on it so that it sounds like a white boy's name.

Frank takes his shirt off and throws it to the sideline. "Listen: Nobody's throwing nothing through nothing," he says. "Let's just play."

"Now *Torta* over here speaks for you?" Similac says.

Similac says everything as a question, so you feel like you're always being tested. Frank's looking at me, trying to bring me back to my senses. But he knows there's no point. He shakes his head and starts walking to the back of the park, where there's a swing set and a broken-down slide. He kicks a bunch of wood chips at some seagulls, and they glide up to the power lines above us. He won't watch. I didn't want him to anyway.

"You worried about him?" Similac asks.

"Me?" I force out a laugh. "Nah."

"How tight was it when Clorox poured bleach in every washer at the Laundromat?"

"Yeah, that *was* tight."

"How cool was it when Shimmy popped the tires on the ice-cream man's truck?"

"Pretty cool."

"That's all it is, just little pranks, you know? You want to do something that dope?"

"Yes!" I say, a little too eagerly. But

immediately I think of the time Omar gave me a bag of ice after Similac threw a ball at the back of my head. I think about how Omar might be one of the nicest guys I've ever met, how he's always letting me have the almost-expired food from his storeroom.

Then Similac puts a hand on my shoulder and gives me a nod. I can't tell if it's straight-up intimidation or if he's saying that this is the beginning of a truly good and mutually beneficial friendship.

I walk over to the demolished church next to the Q Mart. They tore the church down a month after Omar bought the store, and he's always considered it a bad omen. For one, he says, it drove his property value way down. For two, when you tear down

God's house, He reacts the same way you or I would: He gets mad. Omar says that's how Mesopotamia ended—someone tore down a temple they weren't supposed to.

Omar's got his back to the street now. Since the summer started, he's been closing earlier. At the end of every day, he turns around and counts every bottle of unopened alcohol, every pack of unopened cigarettes. Then he logs the results in his notebook. I've seen the pages before: The numbers never change, a bunch of zeroes cascading down his sales column. I look back at the park. Similac's chewing on a stem of grass. He gives a thumbs-up. I step over the little barricade that separates the church from the street and look at the large pile of rubble, searching for an appropriate brick.

An appropriate brick. Even my rebellion smacks of nerdery. What I want is a brick that'll do the job with the least amount of damage. Too big of a brick and it might crush more than the window. Too little of a brick and it could bounce right off the glass. The sweet spot is half a brick, which I find after a little digging at the top of the pile.

I toss the brick back and forth between my hands, feeling its weight, watching the bits of sand and gravel fall between my fingers. I remind myself that it's a dog-eat-dog world out here. I remind myself that technically Iron Man dabbled with the dark side during his Disassembled phase, if only to see what it was like. I remind myself that, all things considered, Omar's not even from here—so what's he really losing?

I walk around to the front of Omar's store and aim for a bottom window panel so the brick will hit the stand of romance novels and stop before doing any more damage. I take comfort in the coward's logic: If I can't be a hero, at least I can be a less-evil villain.

I wind up, cocking the brick behind me. I grip it so hard, it feels like it's pulsing. My body goes into autopilot: I set my feet and take a deep breath, and then another. I grit my teeth, and my arm slings forward on its own. When I let go, I grunt a little because my throw is so hard, it feels like my shoulder is coming out of its socket. I watch as the brick sails through one of the top window panels and directly into a lightbulb and a bunch of open wires dangling from the ceiling. Sparks fly like fireworks. Omar was busy counting the change in his register, but once he sees the flames, he leaps over the counter, takes off his shirt, and tries to jump up and snuff out the fire. He jumps up over and over again, the small paunch of his belly jiggling frantically. It's pointless. Flames quickly swallow up his unused merchandise. I want to help, but everything in my body tells me to run.

I sprint until I'm tired, about a dozen blocks, to a street I've never been on, full of colorful front-yard gardens. The roses are yawning pinks and reds, and some of the bigger oranges hang down from their branches. I take big, desperate breaths.

I could live here, on this block. I could eat plums and oranges for breakfast every morning with a nice family. I could wake up to the sun on my face. On weekends I'd cut the grass, and at night we'd play Jenga together. And nothing bad would ever happen. Ever.

CHAPTER 4

PROOF THAT I AM NOT, IN FACT, PURE EVIL

I keep a list of summer goals under my mattress. I got the idea after reading a *Popular Mechanics* article about some kid in Iowa who made a wind turbine out of recycled book covers or something. Kids like that are supposed to be inspirational, but you end up hating them. They've got everything, and you, who have nothing, have to read about them. But I kept reading long enough to note that the kid said he wrote his goals down every day. Must be something to it, I thought, so I did the same. Here's the unabridged list:

1. Figure out life plans

2. ~~Find a girlfriend~~ Get over that weird nauseous feeling you have when talking to girls

3. Earn respect of peers!

4. Make sure Frank stays out of trouble

5. Earn Zen Master rating in WoW!!

6. Read *Don Quixote*

7. Play a little basketball every day

8. Stop doing that thing where you slump so you don't look as tall

9. Stop doing that thing where you hold on to your old clothes like you'll ever fit in them again

10. ~~Have better relationship with Dad~~ Try to be nicer to Dad when you see him

As you can see, burning down Omar's store is not on that list.

CHAPTER 5
THE FUGITIVE
(STARRING JUSTIN SHAW)

I can already see the headlines:

"Idiot Kid Starts Fire, Kills Hardworking Immigrant"

"Young Thug on Trial for Arson"

"Simpleton Gives In to Peer Pressure, Ruins Life"

When I get home, I run to my room and pack a bag: underwear and socks, a couple pairs of jeans, my favorite Indiana Jones T-shirts. I pack a few comics—early-edition Star Wars stuff, crème de la crème—and then take them out. Extra weight can only slow you down when you're on the run. According to crime novels, you wear dark clothes and pay for things in cash. That's worst case. Preferably, you're sticking to the woods and throwing the hounds off your tracks with cayenne pepper. Best case, you're stealing a boat in some sleepy coastal town and sailing to a new life as a papaya grower in Panama.

Mom calls out from the kitchen, asking me to sit with her and tell her about my day.

We live on West Street, close enough to see the fingers of smoke still coming from the Q Mart. It's one of those narrow-frame houses first owned by the porters back in the day. As I walk down the hallway I keep clear of the windows, built to let the sunlight in. Now these windows seem too low, too transparent. The front door suddenly looks very easy to kick in. In the kitchen, Mr. Hunter stands over the stove frying some fish, while Mom sits at our tiny kitchen table giving him instructions.

"Egg, flour, crumbs," Mom says.

"That's what I'm doing," Mr. Hunter says. "Watch your tone."

"You watch *your* tone. There's crumbs all in the egg."

Mom frowns when she sees me. "Something's wrong," she says.

"The boy's fine," Mr. Hunter says. "Looks good to me."

Mom says, "Since when did you become an expert in how *my* child is doing?"

"Actually, I like to think of him as my child, too."

"Good! You should!"

Mom folds her arms and sits stiffly in her chair. Mr. Hunter turns back to the stove and scoops a blackened piece of fish onto a waiting paper towel.

"How was Bushrod?" Mom asks.

"Fine," I say.

"Something happen? You look like something happened."

"Nah, nothing happened."

Mom's a nurse at Highland Hospital and has the most finely tuned radar for bullshit you've ever seen. Lying to her involves maximum confidence and finesse. She's quick with the belt or shoe or whatever else is lying around. The day after she kicked my dad out, she put all his shit in plastic bags and drove it to Goodwill.

As she lifted the bags out of the trunk, she said it's important to remember that you should never turn off your bullshit detector for anybody.

On the other hand, Mr. Hunter dresses boring, eats boring, talks boring. Even when he's excited, his voice sounds like a fan blowing in an empty room. Since marrying my mom, he's tried to mold me into an All-American boy. Boy Scouts, keyboard lessons, karate, youth brass band, youth choir, African drumming. It's like he thinks I'm some kind of Make-A-Wish kid. He's always signing me up for things he believes will enrich my mind and soul. When I get anything less than a B, he sits me down and tells me stories about the achievements of civil rights leaders.

These are the people whose lives I've just ruined, who will refer to me as the Child Who Shall Not Be Named while I rot in jail on an arson bid.

Mr. Hunter leaves the kitchen and then returns, holding his hands behind his back.

"Your mother and I have been thinking," Mr. Hunter starts. He waits for Mom's approval, and when she nods, he continues.

"I've been noticing how much you go to the park. And we've talked in the past about your growing interest in the game of basketball."

Mr. Hunter is beaming, but all I can feel is dread. I've been lying about my basketball prowess at Bushrod, to try to keep me out of science camp this summer. For all my mom and Mr. Hunter know, I'm a demigod at Bushrod. I regale them with stories of my basketball glory, of hook shots that never happened and dunks that are pure fiction. I give them detailed recollections of games. I walk around the house sometimes practicing fadeaway jumpers and crossovers. The whole basketball thing has excited the hell out of them.

"Obviously," Mr. Hunter says, "I'd rather have you do something more productive with your summer, like pre-algebra at Laney. Maybe some kind of volunteering." Mr. Hunter pauses here with his eyebrows cocked, waiting for a reaction. "Okay, okay. There are other ways of improving yourself, that's what I'm learning."

With a final smile, he moves his hands from behind his back and passes me a black shoe box. I hesitate to take it, but Mr. Hunter gently shoves the box into my hands. It's a new pair of Jordans. The 11s, all the rage this summer. These are the black patent leather joints with white uppers. Size fourteen. I mentioned them a few weeks ago as a part of the whole "Justin Shaw is the King of Bushrod" thing. I didn't actually want them. I was just going for authenticity.

This is bad. Mom doesn't have money for these. Mr. Hunter definitely doesn't have money for these. Mr. Hunter owns a carpet-cleaning business, and from the conversations I overhear at night, business is not going well. I have no idea where this money came from. I imagine Mom going down to the pawn shop and selling one of

Granddad's war medals for half its value. I imagine Mr. Hunter begging for a heavier tip on one of his cleaning jobs.

"You don't like 'em," Mom says.

"I do," I say. "They're dope."

I try them on, and my toes edge up against the front of the shoe. They're perfect. I walk around the kitchen, taking a bunch of showy steps. I hop up and down a little. I do a little fadeaway jumper. Mr. Hunter watches me eagerly. If there was ever a time to feel bad about wearing a pair of two-hundred-dollar shoes, this is it.

I give Mom a hug and shake Mr. Hunter's hand.

"Thank you," I say. "These are really gonna take my game to the next level."

"Whatever you need to do," Mr. Hunter

says, "we're here for you."

"I hope you know," Mom says, "that you wouldn't have those shoes or that shirt or those shorts if your father were around."

For dinner we eat the fish and white bread. I'm so nauseous that even the smell of the fish is about to send me over the edge.

"Let's pray," Mr. Hunter says.

I'm not the praying type, but I play along. We take one another's hands. Mr. Hunter asks for a lot of things. He asks for, amen, strength to be the leader of his home, to be the Moses of our tribe. He asks for, amen, plenty (of what, I don't know). He asks for patience, amen. He asks that, yes, Lord, obedience fall over the house. He asks for the demons of selfishness and immaturity and violence to stay out of this house. He asks that we do the same things in darkness that we'd do in light. He asks that we find the courage to ask for forgiveness in a world that rewards cowards who keep their mouths shut.

"Amen," Mr. Hunter says heavily.

"Amen," Mom says.

"Amen," I say, with more oomph than I expected.

CHAPTER 6
A PART OF MY LIFE YOU PROBABLY WON'T BELIEVE

The day before Pop got himself kicked out for the final time, he took me to Bushrod for our usual game of one-on-one. I was eight. We always played on Saturday mornings. Back then he was in and out all the time, leaving for a few days, coming back for a few. Mom put up with it for a while, would welcome him back and ask no questions about where he'd been, like nothing had happened. Instead, they'd talk about little things, like how the grass needed to be cut or some boards needed fixing. He would touch her on the small of her back, and she would exhale quietly. That's how I knew she was getting fed up. At night she'd bolt the door, which meant that for a few weeks, Pop had to climb the fence and walk around to the back of the house to let himself in through my window.

This particular time it had rained the night before. When he climbed through my window, he made my whole bed wet, and I had to sleep on damp sheets. On the way to the park the next morning, I sprinted and jumped over a big puddle on the sidewalk, knowing that overt displays of athleticism bothered the hell out of him.

"You think jumping high makes you good?" he asked with a trace of anger in his voice.

I shrugged.

"You know how many do-nothing Negroes jump high out here? Guys out here pumping gas that'll dunk on your head. You understand that Moses Malone barely got up off the ground? And he was the greatest of all time. It's about skill."

I jumped over another puddle.

"These are life lessons I'm teaching you," he said. "I'm trying to tell you about life."

That was him all day, every day: always teaching you some kind of lesson you didn't ask for. Always wanting you to understand what it is to be a *man* and expecting you to get the message through the vodka on his breath. "The world," he'd once said, "will try to keep you a black boy your whole life. I'm not raising you to be no hat-in-your-hand Negro. You have to work to become a man." He was one of those adults—along with all teachers, police officers, pastors, counselors, rappers, and politicians—who never practiced what he preached.

When we got to the court, he stood to the side to step out of his Windbreakers. This was his ritual, his way of showing respect to the game. He has a gnarly scar from an old work accident that runs from the top of his knee to the middle of his thigh, and he liked to wear these short shorts to accentuate it. They were Magic Johnson short, and the Warriors logo on the front had faded to just a few yellow lines. I was still a confident kid then, still a couple of years away from sinking into nerdier ambitions. I clowned his shorts, told him they belonged in a museum.

"You can start telling me how to dress for basketball when you beat me at basketball," he said.

We never warmed up or shot around. The game was always to twenty-one. A lot of the way he played depended on whether he liked me in that particular moment. If I hadn't messed up or gotten into trouble at school, if I could go a week without a vice principal leaving a voice mail, it was all laughter and wild hook shots. He'd let me get the score close and then pull away with a few timely jumpers. But if I was messing up, if I'd brought home anything less than a B or in some way disgraced the family name, he'd play hard and cheat. The game would become a kind of punishment.

That day I couldn't tell what kind of mood he was in. He shot for takeout and missed, grumbling to himself. I held the ball at the top of the key, and he stood around the free-throw line. He was crouching, his arms wide, his scar dark and stretched, with a smart-ass smirk on his face. He was daring me to shoot, knowing that I was a streaky. Some days I made five or six in a row, but some days I couldn't hit the rim. I never practiced unless he was with me. Without taking a dribble, I drained three jumpers in a row. Nine–nothing.

"You won't keep that up," he said, creeping a little closer to me.

We'd been playing since I could walk, and I'd never beaten him. He bought me a Fisher-Price rim for my fifth birthday. He set it up in the living room and spent the entire day backing me down and dunking on me. When I started to cry, he threatened a spanking.

On my next jumper I missed left. An air ball. The ball rolled into the grass.

"See," he said, wiping the dew off the ball, "that's what happens when you try to do too much. That's what I've been saying. You try to play like a pro, but you don't know the first thing about fundamentals."

Out came his bag of tricks. When we watched basketball at home, he'd try to teach me how to watch the game. Really *watch* it.

"You think you're watching the game," he'd say, "but you really ain't."

He'd say the game wasn't won or lost

in the highlights. "For example," he'd say, "look at the way that guy in the post got that offensive rebound." He'd jump off the couch and sit on the floor right in front of the TV, his finger on the screen. "That was no accident. That guy put a forearm into his defender's chest, which threw the defender off balance for just a half a second. That's all you need."

As he drove to the basket, he shoved a forearm in my chest so hard that I stumbled back underneath the basket. He watched me hit the post, then scooted a bit closer and tossed a dainty floater off the backboard and in.

"Bird-chested," he said, walking back to the three-point line. "Play bigger. You haven't been doing your push-ups."

On defense he gave me a solid punch in the gut when I took jumpers. The score was 17–10, him. His hands were on his knees between points, and big sweat blots ran down the front and back of his shirt. His shirt collar yawned, and I could make out some dark spots on his neck. You could see a whole lot of bad nights written on his face.

"I'm gonna win," I said. It was my ball, and I stood at the top of the key.

"Overconfidence," he said. "The calling card of the prima donna."

I drove hard right, and then put the ball behind my back as I went left, something I'd seen on TV once. But I couldn't get a good grip and fumbled the ball out of bounds.

Pop said nothing. Probably he was too disappointed to talk smack. He limped to the three-point line. Slowly he started backing me down. I could smell the sweat and deodorant and beer from the night before on him. I could hear him wheeze. Without turning around, he tossed a hook shot over both of our heads, and it went off the backboard and in. A miracle if you've ever seen one. Instead of celebrating, he walked quietly back to the three-point line, his hands folded over the back of his head.

It was game point. The sun was just starting to peek out through the clouds. Starting at the top of the key, he backed me down slowly, throwing all his weight against me. He put up another little hook shot. It went in again. Again, he didn't celebrate. He picked the ball up, walked to the sideline, and put his pants on.

Maybe deep down I knew that was the last time we'd play, because I was mad as hell. On the way home I wouldn't even talk to him. When he tried to put his arm around me, I walked ahead of him.

"Somebody die?" he asked.

"No," I said.

"Then what you all mad for? That's life, and I don't care if you want to hear it. You'll get your ass kicked sometimes, and you'll have to deal with that. Sometimes you're the hammer, sometimes you're the nail."

CHAPTER 7

THERE ARE SURPRISES AND THEN THERE ARE SURPRISES

All things considered, it could be worse. No one was hurt, and the store didn't burn down completely. On the news they like to pan the camera over the Q Mart, pausing on the money shots, the water-damaged roof, the blown-out windows, jagged shards of glass stuck in the frames like shark teeth.

Do I feel horrible? Of course I do. I watch Omar from the park. He's set up a little plastic table just outside of the Q Mart, and every few minutes he organizes and reorganizes it. From the looks of things, he's selling all the knicknacks he could salvage: waterlogged rolls of toilet paper, smudged lotto tickets, ballpoint pens, cigarillos.

But for now I put that out of my mind.

I've returned to Bushrod triumphantly. I'm wearing my new Js; on the way over, I walked stiffly so I wouldn't crease them. It seems to me that summer is starting today, right now. When I get there, Similac's at half-court picking teams. I walk up to him, ready to hear my praises sung, ready to be anointed to—

"You really thought we were gonna let you play?" he says.

"What?" I say.

"You seen what you done? You didn't see the dude's store?"

"But. Why did you—"

"Would you hang out with you if you were us?"

My head is spinning. "You said— I was just— You told me to."

"Oh." Similac cracks his knuckles. "We had a gun to your head?"

Similac puts his hand on my back and pushes me to the side of the court so they can start the game.

"Dope kicks, though," he says.

It's been two weeks now, and we're back to the same routine. The police haven't come for me, but if they do, I've made peace with it. I'll take my punishment when it comes. Frank says that because I don't have a record, I probably won't do any time. But if I do, he says they'll probably send me to the cuddlier YA Camp, the kind for kids who miss school or yell at their moms. For now I sit in the grass and read *Don Quixote*. Omar gave it to me a while back. It's all about how we sometimes blur the line between fantasy and reality, confusing one for the other. I won't lie, most of it's hella boring—too many references to fine cloths and mutton—but I'm committed to finishing it. I want to walk across the street to talk to him about it, but every time I see him yawn and look at his watch, I lose courage.

The guys have been playing extra hard recently, sometimes staying after dark. They do it on Similac's orders. There's some talk of the boys from Ghosttown coming down to play us in a couple of weeks. One of the guys from Ghosttown came up to Fat Jimmy at Ray's Barbers and challenged us to a game. Fat Jimmy said everyone in the shop was looking at him, so he had to accept. But if you ask me, he just signed our death certificate. The kids from Ghosttown are killers. Big, fast, strong—they live to play outdoor ball during the summer. No AAU for them. No referees and free throws interrupting the flow of the game. They show up to your neighborhood like Vikings—ready to conquer, pillage, and plunder. If the rumors are to be believed, they'll strip the losing team of their shoes after the game. They will invite the losing team's girlfriends to pie at Nation's. They will claim ownership of your park, make you pay a tax on it for playing.

Everyone knows we don't stand a chance, but Similac has everyone practicing out here like we do. He draws up nonsense plays in the dirt like the leader of a guerrilla army. No one knows what he's talking about. Whenever he walks to the water fountain, the other kids grumble about how he's not even funny anymore.

It's another hot-ass nothing day until Frank notices the two girls watching us from the other side of the fence. Frank's got a third eye for the females, like some kind of radar for the X chromosome. It took a minute for all of us to catch on. When I turned back to Frank, he was smoothing down the five or six whiskers under his nose, a little island of hair he calls a mustache. After the smoothing came some jutting of his chin toward the street. I thought he was motioning toward Omar, so I didn't look. Someone asked Frank what his problem was. When none of us got the hint, Frank sighed, deep and dramatic. He jutted his chin harder, more obviously, and we followed it like a compass.

The girls are all the way across the blacktop. When it's this hot, with the heat pressing down on your neck like an iron, everything looks ten times farther away than it really is. The girls look like they might be a hundred miles away, maybe farther, like they're out in the Mojave somewhere. I imagine myself walking to them, the soles of my shoes melting into the concrete, my thirst unquenchable.

"Water," I will gasp as I reach them.

"So heroic," they will say, carrying me back to their lair.

They've got their fingers wrapped around the chain-link like vines, and even from this far you can tell they probably smell like something amazing.

It's rare we're blessed with flesh-and-blood girls at the court. Every day's a dude fest. One time Frank brought his cousin, who was from LA but starting her first year at Cal State East Bay. Her sunglasses were all Hollywood, big and dark, and she was wearing the kind of short shorts that would break a Negro's heart. Plus she had on these fly-girl earrings that glinted wildly in the sun. The kind of girl so dope, she makes you think about every single one of your faults, every reason she'd have to reject you. I was having trouble not staring, so I focused on a spot of brown grass between my legs. She sat next to me, dug her fingers into the warm dirt, and pulled out a dandelion.

"It's pretty," she said, turning it around in her fingers. Yellow petals fell onto her wrist.

"You're pretty," I murmured, not looking up. I tried to play it cool, tried to ignore the sweat rolling down my back.

"Thanks," she said. "I need to ask Frank something real quick." She walked over to Frank and never came back. For the rest of the afternoon, I traced the outline her butt had made in the dirt next to me.

The girls are whispering to each other now, the bottoms of their braids fluttering behind them in the breeze. One of them's tall and skinny-armed, her skin dark and shiny in the sun. Now she's standing with one sneaker hooked in the fence. If I didn't know any better, I'd say she's at least as tall as I am. You never see girls that tall.

When she talks to her friend (sister?), they cup their hands over their mouths. What are they saying? Who knows. They're probably exchanging secrets.

Frank likes to remind me that I have technically never had a girlfriend, and he's not wrong. There was some brief hand-holding with Tara Wiley in the fourth grade, a glorious week that she suddenly can't remember now that we're in high school. There was also the time Ashley Mayfield blew an eyelash off my cheek in the seventh grade. Her lips got real close to my face and almost brushed my skin. When I told Frank that story, how I thought it was a sign of things to come, he got this embarrassed look on his face like he wasn't sure he'd heard me right. But what does he know about unspoken body language? After school he takes girls into an empty science lab and comes out fifteen minutes later with a smile that would rip an average kid's face apart.

"Would you lovely damsels enjoy a closer look?" Frank shouts to the girls.

"Of what?" the tall girl says.

Frank dribbles the ball once and gets ready to shoot. It seems only fair that he should miss. I'm not saying this out of malice, but it's just that Frank already has a dozen girls texting him at all hours of the day.

When's the nerdboy going to get a chance? Who's looking out for me? So I'm praying that Frank misses and maybe lands awkwardly on his ankle, and in a heroic twist, I have to carry him to safety. As Frank lies in the hospital, clinging to life, I'll take the girls for ice cream, somewhere cozy where our bare knees touch under the table.

But no, it isn't meant to be. The ball spins through the rim, barely grazing it. Frank lands and is fine. He does a kind of fist pump and takes a small victory lap around the court. I feel a little bit of shame, but mostly disappointment.

"And?" the tall girl says, unimpressed. She's almost laughing as she says it, her braces flashing for a second before she closes her mouth. From my spot on the grass, I laugh a little, too. So maybe there's hope. We are laughing *together*.

"If I do it again," Frank says, "you will grace me with your number."

Then, a hip thrust: Frank actually does a hip thrust.

"Do it again," the tall girl says.

Despite everything that happened with Omar, I still believe that there are times in life when one must take a chance. Throughout history, great men have taken risks. I get up from the grass and wipe the dirt off my hands. I walk over to the court, my steps feeling heavy, powerful. I grab the ball and run my fingers over it. I will shoot it and I will make it; the girls and I will get ice cream. We will go to the movies at Jack London. We will sit in the back, in the darkest, most private row. Then we will sacrifice ourselves to our bodies' hunger.

Frank grabs me by the arm and pulls me to the sideline for a conference.

"The hell are you doing?" he hisses.

"Taking charge," I say. "Ergo, winning the hearts of these fair ladies."

"Don't," he whispers hoarsely. He squints. I scored in the ninety-fifth percentile in state testing, but Frank hates it when I break out the vocabulary big guns. "I'm doing this. I got it."

I look over to the girls. I'm hoping that in my eyes they see a kind of steely resolve.

"Please," Frank says, turning away from the fence so the girls can't see what he's saying. "They're into me. I'm this close." He holds his fingers up a half inch apart.

"They were laughing at you," I say.

"With me, my dude. With me."

"I got this," I say.

He tries to grab the ball, but I hold it over my head. Frank jumps for it once and then gives up. I walk to half-court as the rest of the guys on the court back up, giving me some space. There are murmurs, chuckles, especially from Similac. Of course, great men were often chuckled at. Jesus. Buddha. Marcus Garvey. All bullied.

A breeze rattles a chain of some kind, metal-on-metal somewhere far away. I stare at the little square in the middle of the backboard. My hands are sweating; I wipe them on my shorts. There's a little tremor in my leg, maybe a nervous muscle. I take a step forward and cock the ball near my ear, the way my dad used to teach me. As I shoot the ball I think back to the games we used to play, how he enjoyed whipping me, talking shit all the way home. Then it occurs to me that maybe this isn't a good idea. The ball is flying to the rim on an arc that seems a little too high, it's moving a little too fast, it is aiming for a rim that is much farther away.

I can hear Frank moan as the ball sails over the backboard and into the grass. The other guys on the court shake their heads. It is too sad a situation for laughter. I've ruined everyone's fantasy. Tonight, brothers, dads, and uncles will hear this story; it will be used as a lesson for future generations. Do not let an egghead near your athletic equipment. Keep him away from your womenfolk. An empty McDonald's cup rolls away from an overflowing garbage can and tumbles toward the fence. When I look over, the girls are gone, beamed up to wherever they came from.

It's Fat Jimmy who suggests that I should play the kids from Ghosttown. It's obviously a sad little attempt at redemption, an effort to save himself from falling to the very bottom of the totem pole. It suddenly occurs to me that this is probably how the world has always worked, in every neighborhood, village, and city. Save the town by sacrificing its weak and vulnerable to the invading hordes. I come along and throw Omar under the bus, and then Fat Jimmy gets his chubby fingers around my neck and does the same to me. I get it. Similac summons me from the grass and asks me what I think.

I look around the circle. Faces grin back at me eagerly. Everyone except Frank, who's just shaking his head. But the way I see it, I've got nothing to lose. The way I see it, I've already hit rock bottom. The only place to go is up.

"Yeah, I'll play them," I say.

A couple of forced whoops come up from the crowd.

"Who wants to be on my team?" I ask.

"Whoa," Similac says. "Whoa, whoa, whoa. Who said anything about us playing with you? This should be about you making good, right? You know, bring some positivity back to the neighborhood after everything that happened?" He points across the street.

A couple of guys shake their heads at the memory of the burning Q Mart. Omar is sitting at his little table, pressing the dark circles under his eyes.

Frank gets up and brushes the dirt off his butt.

"Forget y'all," he says, and motions for us to walk away. Which is how I know he really is my brother.

CHAPTER 9
HOW TO START YOUR OWN DREAM TEAM

We walk through the neighborhood now, strategizing. A couple of beer-soaked older guys walk past us. Ms. Mayfair is out smoking on her porch, the smoke slowly curling above her head. Back in the day, Pop built the wheelchair ramp for her house.

"What are you boys up to?" she asks. Nosy, as always.

"Nothing much," Frank says. "Putting together a basketball team. You wanna play?"

"Ha! Even if I could walk, I wouldn't play with y'all."

"Plenty of kids we could ask to play," Frank says to me as we cross the street.

After some thought, we've narrowed our list down to a few kids. Long shots for sure, but with the way things are looking, it's either them or nothing.

First stop: Adrian Whately. Frank says he sold Adrian a package of stolen sketch pencils once, and he remembered that Adrian had calves like oranges. A quiet kid, Frank says. His school: unknown. His interests: unknown. We're across the street from Children's Hospital, outside a fortress. Frank says Adrian lives here. The house is separated from the street by a ten-foot steel gate with serrated spears on top. A huge oak tree in the middle of the yard stands guard. All the windows have bars on them.

"How do we know he'll play?" I ask.

"We don't. Got any better ideas?" Frank says.

Frank grabs a broken branch and rattles it across the gate until a woman comes outside.

She's a big woman with little eyes set deep into her face, and she gathers a whole head of steam as she walks out toward us. She's holding a broom in her hand.

"What you banging on my gate for?" she asks. With one hand she grabs the gate, and with her other hand she holds the broom like a sword, the wooden edge pointed directly at Frank's stomach.

"Hi," Frank says, not moving. "Adrian home?"

"No," she says. But behind her, we can

see someone peeking through the curtains.

"Okay," Frank says. "We're his friends. Can you deliver a communication for us?"

"No," she says.

"Just tell him we need to talk to him."

As quickly as she stormed outside, she storms right back in.

"Now what?" I ask.

Frank says he didn't plan on this particular outcome. I look up at the pointed spikes on top of the fence. An invading army couldn't get over them.

We come back the next day.

"I found out that girl was his older sister," Frank says. "Just gotta throw on the charm."

This time she doesn't leave her

doorway. But she's dressed in a frilly yellow dress that stops just above the knee, the kind Mom wore when she first started dating Mr. Hunter. Her bright red lipstick is a shock around her mouth.

"Did I tell you to come back?" she says to us, laughing harshly. There is something in her voice, though, a tone I imagine flirting to sound like. "I already have one little boy here. Don't need two more."

"Who's little?" Frank asks, also laughing, and I have a feeling they're speaking in a language I don't quite understand.

"So young," she says, slamming the door.

Last shot. Frank picks me up tonight. I'm in a Predator sweatshirt, and he's completely dolled up in a black dress shirt, khaki pants, and his one pair of good shoes—Doc Martens. His hair is gelled back. He's got an eye-watering amount of Axe body spray on. I have to admit: He looks like he owns a Macy's card or at least a very nice used car. On the way here he said that he'd usually get to Adrian via simple breaking and entering, but this job's going to require a little more finesse.

"I have doubts about this," I say.

"I'm not wearing my good clothes for nothing," Frank says.

"I am not a supporter of this plan."

"Just do what we talked about."

Frank rakes a fallen branch across the fence. Sure enough, Adrian's sister opens the door and plants one thick hip in the door frame. Her head's wrapped in a satiny nightcap, the kind with a million slippery colors. Her nightgown is wrapped snugly around her.

"Let's talk," Frank says, his voice deep. "I got something very important I want to speak to you about."

"I told you two to stop coming," she says coyly.

"Last time. Promise. After we have our talk."

Adrian's sister furrows her brow. She tucks a stray hair back into her headwrap; with her other hand, she carefully smoothes the front of her nightgown. She looks back into the house and takes a careful step out of the door frame. If I weren't standing right next to Frank, I wouldn't believe it.

Not in a million years.

"So?" Frank asks sweetly.

"I don't know," she says, and something in her voice sounds genuinely unsure.

"Let's talk without all this gate business."

Would you believe me if I told you she walked down the little weedy path that led to the fence, swishing her hips, eyeing Frank like he was a piece of steak? Would you believe me if I told you she opened the gate?

As soon as Frank walks in, he sits on the big leather recliner in the corner like he owns the place. I take a spot on the edge of the couch. Being in here feels like a hall of mirrors, where there are doubles and triples of everything. Everything is floral: the wallpaper, the couch covers, the carpet, the place mats on the dining table.

A small bowl of potpourri sits on top of the TV. On the walls are pictures of Adrian and his sister. One of them at a birthday party, one of them on some kind of fishing trip, one of them at an A's game. Adrian looks less and less happy in the photos, and by the time he's sitting behind a thirteenth birthday cake, he looks furious. When his sister walks into the kitchen to grab us some lemonade, I mouth, *Let's leave.* Frank gives two thumbs up, smiles big and wide.

"Adrian!" Adrian's sister says. "Your friends are here."

A minute later Adrian comes out from a bedroom in the back of the house. He's muscle-y, about five five, and his body looks tense. He's the kind of jumpy kid you can tell has never had any privacy, who's always expecting someone to burst through the door. It's true about his calves—for whatever reason, they bulge out from under his jeans like jet packs. He's got a Green Lantern comic under his arm.

"My old buddy," Frank says. "Where you been?"

"Who are you?" Adrian says. His voice comes out froggy, like he's not used to talking.

"It's me. Frank. The guy who sold you those pencils."

Adrian scratches the back of his neck. "Those pencils were shit."

"I thought you guys knew each other," Adrian's sister says, her eyes narrowing.

Frank is sweating. "We do!"

"You lying to me?"

"Hey," I say, "is that a Green Lantern comic?"

"Yes," Adrian says.

"You mind if I take a look?"

Reluctantly he hands it to me.

I say, "A lot of people don't know that the Green Lantern hated Batman."

Frank rolls his eyes. Adrian's sister yawns.

"Did *you* know," Adrian says, perking up, "his girl was supposed to be Wonder Woman?"

"Superman would've never let that happen."

"Never."

And that's all it takes. Twenty minutes of talking about the genius of Stan Lee and it's like we're old friends. But does he want to play ball with us?

"Yes," his sister says, eyeing Frank. "He needs to get out of the house anyway."

One player down, two more to go. We turn down Seventh and enter a small plaza in Chinatown.

"There's no way White Mike's here," I tell Frank.

"Trust me," Frank says.

"He moved away."

"That's what he wants you to think."

About thirty Chinese guys line up in a perfect square. At the end of one row is Mike, in these baby-blue linens that billow softly in the breeze. He stands with his feet together, his hands straight up in the air, a picture of perfect serenity. His blond hair floats loosely around his head like a cape. Still, he has the kind of bulky frame you might expect from a good rebounder.

Technically everybody knows White Mike. For three years he was the brawny, mohawked love interest of the main character on a Disney series for preteens. He was always getting his broad shoulders adorably stuck in a doorway or window, his attempts at love foiled by comical accidents. Let's just say fame was not kind to him. Rumor had it that he left the show, moved out to a farm in Montana. Truth is, he moved back in with his parents in Oakland.

Frank walks right in front of Mike so that he's standing between Mike and the crowd.

"We need to talk," he says.

"Peace," Mike says in the hushed tone of a librarian. He takes a moment to look Frank in the eye and smile warmly, and then he turns to me and does the same. He strikes me as the kind of person who would hug you for no reason.

"It's urgent," Frank says.

"Release that urgency," Mike says. "Release that stress."

Frank turns to me. I shrug. Around us, the men begin to lie down. Some of them, because they are so old, have to do it in stages, folding into themselves like pieces of paper.

Mike lies flat on his back, his arms at his sides, the soles of his feet touching. His eyes are closed. Technically I was a little older than the show's target audience, but

I still watched. It's a secret I planned to take to the grave. My favorite episode is the one where Mike discovers a time machine that can take him back to the moment he and his crush first met, only to learn that his head is too big for the machine's safety helmet.

"Mike?" I say. "You there?"

"I'm here," he whispers.

"I'm Justin," I say.

"It's a pleasure."

"I thought you were good on that show."

Frank gives me a look, his mouth partially open.

"A different life, my friend," Mike says. "A past life."

"How's this life?"

Mike opens his eyes. "Wonderful."

"Bullshit," Frank interrupts. "You've been

in hiding for, like, two years."

"And in that time I've found peace," Mike says defensively. He gets up and bends deeply, his arms stretched awkwardly behind his back.

This is going nowhere. I tell Frank we should leave. I tell him that an object at rest stays at rest, and in Mike we have a rested object. Instead, Frank grabs a fistful of Mike's collar.

"Okay," Frank says. "Look: We have a basketball team. You're going to join it. If you don't, I'll tell everyone your schedule and your phone number, and you'll go back to having kids jumping on your back at Walmart."

"Easy," Mike says, trying to free himself. "Let's be easy."

"We start practice tomorrow night," Frank says. "And if you're not there, I'm putting your address on the Internet."

Mike lets out a sigh.

Frank says, "I'm glad we've come to an understanding."

Later that afternoon I see Pop. Frank and I are walking below an overpass on our way to find some kid Frank sold a little weed to once. Rumor has it he might be a baller, too. Above us, cars rumble loudly, on their way to destinations unknown. We're still on a high from seeing Mike, not paying attention, shouting, listening to our voices bounce off the concrete. It feels like everything is finally coming together. Then two guys step to us. They're both my height, but older-looking. Their hoodies and jeans look too thick for the heat.

"Yo," one of them says.

"'Sup," Frank says.

"I like that chain you got," the other one of them says, nodding to Frank. His eyes seem to glow when he says *chain*.

Frank has been jumped before, but other than a couple shove fests as a kid, I've got no fighting experience. My first instinct is to look for escape routes. Immediately I think of the way Omar was always talking about how karma is the one true universal rule, how what goes around comes around, and there is no escaping that. I start imagining worst-case scenarios, sneaker marks implanted deeply on the side of my face, a life of nothing but pureed carrots to eat. I look at Frank, hoping he'll give his chain up, even though I know he won't. I can see the veins in his neck popping, his fists curling, and that's when Pop and his two friends walk up behind the kids, towering over them like sentries.

"Whoa, whoa, whoa," Pop says, a two-by-four in his hand. He doesn't yell but speaks just above the roar of the traffic above us. "Did you know that in some cultures, petty theft is punishable by death? An irony, when one thinks about it, but one that I think makes sense given man's impulse to dominate his fellow man."

Pop's friends laugh gruffly behind him. Pop has no shirt on, and his belly hangs over his pants. His two friends, in their combat boots, stand with their shoulders thrown back, cracking their knuckles. They look different from the day we saw them at McDonald's. A moment passes in which the two kids assess their chances against Pop and his friends, and then decide against it. They push past Frank and me and keep walking.

"A bully," Pop says, dusting his hands, "is just a coward with toned biceps."

"I didn't need your help," I say. "We coulda handled it."

"Didn't look like it," Pop says.

"Nothing looks right when you're drunk."

"Stone-cold sober, my boy."

I start to walk away.

"Usually," Pop says, "in these situations, one owes their hero a favor."

"Why would I do you a favor?" I ask.

"Yup," Pop says, ignoring me. "Just a quick game. I'll come pick you up soon."

THE LAKE

Frank and I spend days looking for a fifth player. We even make the mistake of going to Ray's Barbers. He stops in the middle of a haircut to scold us.

"What are you on?" he asks. Ray thinks all kids are on drugs.

"We're gonna win," I say.

"That must be the drugs talking. What is it, PCP? Is that what y'all do now? Here's what you do: You tell everybody your grandma in Texas got sick and you're going to spend the summer there. Then you lay low for a month, maybe two."

Rumors swirl about the Ghosttown team. They took the Greyhound down to LA and beat a team from Leimert Park just for fun. One day they are all seven footers with size twenty-two shoes. The next day they are a squad of five LeBron James–size teens.

On our mission to find more players, we end up at the lake.

If there's anyone with enough balls to play on our team, it's the guys who play there. There's almost no chance they say yes, so I don't have my hopes up. These guys have bodies like Optimus Prime, crazily sculpted chest muscles and crazy big legs. Guys who look like they stay in the gym twenty-four/seven. Veins popping aggressively out of their biceps. We're looking for anyone young enough to play with us. Frank and I watch the end of one game from the bleachers. The sun is setting in a glorious way, orange spreading out over the water like a spill. People are lined up around the court, shoulder to shoulder. The court is a thing of beauty: perfect lines, perfect white nets hanging off the rims. The kids with the freshest Js stand under the basket, clearing a little space between them and everyone else. I look down at my outfit—old Chucks and a Legion of Doom T-shirt—and feel like someone's going to ask me to leave.

The teams are tied at nineteen, two points away from game. A bald-headed dude brings the ball up the court. He's been killing the entire game. He's all brute strength and speed, a blur once he gets going into the lane. He drives into the lane, and his defender backs off him. But then the guy shoots a jumper, which is a big mistake, because he can't shoot at all. He air-balls it right into the hands of a guy from the other team, who's laughing. In fact, his whole team is laughing. It takes me a second to realize that they baited the guy into shooting the jumper, and he fell for it.

"That guy sucks," Frank says.

"Nah," I say. "That was just smart defense."

The point guard dribbles down the court with 100 percent control. On the whole, his team is older than the team they're playing against. Their arms are still ripped, but they look a little softer. The point guard passes the ball into the post, to this guy with goggles who hasn't shot all game. He's at least six five, and he's got that grown-man's beard. For some reason, he's being guarded by this short, stout guy. He looks to pass to the wing, the same pass he's made all game, but he fakes it and turns to the basket for a hook shot. Game over. The losing team walks off, yelling at each other for letting the game slip away.

"Hey, Frank," I say. "Did you see that? That was all strategy."

"I wish I could get ripped like that."

Frank suggests we ask one of the players to be on our team. Maybe the tall, goggled guy. Maybe the little Hulk on the other team. He says they looked like the best players.

Now that the game's over, the teams playing the next game step onto the court. And that's when I see her, the tall girl from Bushrod the other day. She stands under the basket and tosses in a couple of lay-ups with each hand. Then she slowly moves away from the basket, and after a few minutes, she's all the way out behind the arc. Her hair is in a ponytail that runs down her back and shakes side to side every time she puts up a jumper. Her form is perfect: back straight, feet pointed toward the rim, elbow in close. It's the kind of form that would make my dad cry out with delight. She sends the ball on its way with a quick flick of the wrist. It arcs high in the air and spins like it's on some planetary axis before dropping straight through the net. She's draining shots again and again; the ball barely hits the net and makes the kind of splashing sound that travels all the way around the court. None of the guys on the court talk to her.

We're almost the same height, but somehow the girl seems more comfortable standing there. When she's not shooting, her arms hang easily at her sides. I move through the crowd and stand on her side of the court. She's not even looking at anything except the rim, as if none of us are here. When she shoots, she runs after the ball, brings it back to the three-point line, and starts again. I count five dudes warming up with her. Mostly they're older guys, with fading arm tattoos and chests that look both hard and soft at the same time.

It's only after someone shoots for takeout that they realize there are eleven people on the court.

"I had next," the girl says.

"Yeah," a guy with a headband says. "You got *next next*."

"Nah, I've been here," she says. "You can have next next."

"AJ," the dude says, turning to someone else, "who had next?"

"Pretty sure you did," AJ says.

At which point I feel it's necessary I step in, if for no other reason than the fact that Don Quixote would've done the same.

"Sirs," I say, "I believe the lady had next."

And next thing I know, I've been punched in the head, knocked to the ground, and from what I can gather, there's a scrambling as phones are pulled out. Various *OHHHH*s ring and echo all around me. The ground is liquid under me. I feel myself being half dragged to the side of the court. As I try to get up, there's more commotion, and I know intuitively that Frank has jumped in from the sidelines to raise hell. But these are grown men, not high-school kids, and as I'm about to get up, Frank comes flying into me. We both fall into the bleachers.

I can almost hear the Internet cables surging as people upload their videos.

I have to hold Frank back for his own good. As we walk back to the water fountains, I tell him he's got blood running out of his nose.

"Fuck you," he says. "So do you."

There's a throbbing around my right eye. As I splash cold water on it, I can hear the ball bouncing back and forth up the court. They've started the game without her. But after a couple of minutes, Frank's laughing. He says anyone who's never lost a fight has never really fought. It's almost pitch black at this end of the park. A tallish figure walks up to us. I can feel Frank tense up.

"That was dumb," the girl says. Not what I was expecting to hear.

"Yeah, thanks a lot," Frank says. "We were trying to help you."

"Don't need anybody's help. This stuff happens to me all the time. I'm used to it."

"Whatever," Frank says. He moves closer to her in the dark. "You were at

Bushrod the other day."

"Yeah," she says. She says she lives in Sacramento during the school year but stays with her grandmother during the summer to work at her store in Fruitvale. At night she tries to find a few runs, but no one will let her on. She's tried everywhere. She came to Bushrod with her cousin to check it out and see what kinds of players we had. She wasn't impressed.

"You're a lot finer with jeans on," Frank says.

She smacks her lips.

And do you know what I do next? I start to cry. A big massive level-five hurricane of gulps and tears and snot. Think about everything that's happened in the past two weeks: I've burned down a good friend's store, duped my mom and stepdad into buying me shoes I know they can't afford, and just gotten my ass kicked in front of a girl I'd never met but am already in love with.

"Yo," Frank says. "You crying?"

"Nah," I say, pretending to blow my nose into my shirt.

"Yeah, man. You are."

"Frank! Goddamn it!"

My eye's just about swollen shut, but in the darkness I can feel her looking at me. Somehow, I know it's the kind of look you give to a bird with a broken wing. I'm sure she'll never be into me, not with the two first impressions I've given her. But, in a way, it's liberating. Now I don't have to worry about being this Casanova, this man of a thousand women. And that feeling is kind of nice, I guess. Kind of freeing.

"Janae," she says.

"Justin," I say.

With nothing left to lose, I tell her everything. I tell her about the boys from Ghosttown, how they'll probably beat us and suck our spirits from our bodies. I tell her we've got no chance. I tell her about White Mike and Adrian, how they might not even play but that they're the best we got. I tell her I'm the worst.

"I'll play," she says, shrugging. "When do we practice?"

The next morning Pop shows up at the house. He's yelling at Mom through the door, asking if she would consider taking him back. He's completely sloshed, I can tell. He's singing random lyrics from Barry White songs. From my room I can hear Mom say that if he doesn't get off the property, she's going to call the police.

"Babe!" Pop shouts.

"Don't babe me," Mom says.

"Don't babe my wife," Mr. Hunter says.

"Who died and made you king?" Pop says.

"You did," Mr. Hunter says, "when you left this family."

"I did not leave this family via free will."

Mr. Hunter snorts. "Well, you shouldn't even be here right now."

"Why not open this door and tell me what I should or shouldn't do to my face?"

Mr. Hunter has the spindly legs of a long-distance runner; no doubt Pop would crush him like an empty soda can if things ever got physical. But with Mom standing there, Mr. Hunter says maybe he will open the door. Maybe he'll open the door and show Pop what a real man is. Pop laughs and says he's waiting. Mr. Hunter says he's sure that's what he would want, for him to go to jail on an assault charge and leave Mom wide open for the taking.

Mom says she no one's freaking property.

"Sorry," Mr. Hunter says, slinking back to their bedroom.

It goes on like this all morning. Mom calls the police, but they never come.

"*I've heard people sayyyy,*" Pop sings, "*toooo much of anything ain't good for you.*"

I put on my shorts and Chucks and head for the door.

"And where do you think you're going?" Mom asks.

"It's a long story," I say.

Mom gives me a look. *The look.*

"He got me out of a tight spot the other day. He says I owe him."

"Owe him what? He's your father. That's what he's *supposed* to do."

"Does it sound like he's leaving?"

"So what are you going to do?" Mom asks.

"I'm going to make sure he doesn't come back."

When I get outside, I eye Pop warily. The smell of beer cuts through the smells of the early morning. He puts his hands up to show he means no harm. We walk in silence for a few blocks. He walks out in front of me, sometimes reaching up to slap a stop sign. A garbage truck pulls up next to us, and burly guys in neon vests fling giant bags of trash into the compactor. Pop pulls a cigarette out of his pocket.

"Want one?" he asks.

"No," I say.

"Just testing you."

When we get to Bushrod, Dad takes his coat off, folding it delicately and laying it under the basket we used to play on. In the movies, this is the part where you play against your dad, where you hash things out, maybe settle old scores with the most intense game either of you have ever played. Afterward he moves back in, reunites with Mom, and you guys live happily ever after.

"Let's play to twenty-one," Pop says.

He pulls a partially deflated ball out from under a bench nearby. Pop dribbles it through his legs and lays it up.

"It's a little on the flat side, but it works. So are you playing or not?" he asks, breathing hard.

"Why won't you leave me alone?" I ask.

He doesn't answer. Instead, he steps

behind the three-point line and shoots. He waits a second, then cheers when the ball goes in.

"One game of twenty-one," he says. "Then I'll leave you alone."

"Whatever."

He checks the ball to me, and I check it back to him. He shoots, almost from half-court.

"Three—nothing," he says.

I find myself playing harder. I don't know why, but I go for blocks and steals. I back him down. I elbow him in the chest and back.

"Game point," I say, checking the ball to him.

His shirt is soaked all the way through. He's wheezing. He peels his hands off his knees to check the ball back.

When I drive around him, he doesn't even move. I raise my hands when I lay it up like Champion of the World.

"That's it," I say. "Leave me alone. Don't talk to me; don't ask me to play ball again."

Pop sits down heavily. He leans over and spits out blood. He's laughing. "It was never about ball, Justin. Never."

CHAPTER 11
AN UPDATE ON OMAR

I think about Omar a lot. I dream about him, actually. He appears in my dreams sometimes right in the middle of the sky, like the moon, his face brown and unhappy. Sometimes in other dreams, I'm running through dark woods, tripping over branches and running into tree trunks. There's somebody hunting me, and I know it's him. It's possible I might have this dream for the rest of my life.

A few days ago it rained unexpectedly, and the last of Omar's shit was soaked through. He sat there in the rain, not moving. After the storm passed, he packed up all his stuff into a grocery bag, leaving only the plastic folding table, which someone had snagged by the next morning. Frank says Omar went back to Nigeria, but I don't want to believe him. I want to believe that there's still time to fix things; I want to believe that it's possible to undo things you wish you'd never done.

CHAPTER 12
ALL-STARS

At night, my crack team of ballers gets together. By then the kids at Bushrod are gone. The trash from their games circles the court like remnants of a wasteful civilization. We are a sad collection of talent, horribly out of place under the court's floodlights. Adrian doesn't have basketball shorts, so he wears jeans. White Mike is always looking over his shoulder, expecting someone to notice him. Janae scowls at everything except the rim, which, in secret moments, she almost smiles at.

On the first night, Frank and I stood to the side and watched Janae, Adrian, and Mike warm up. They said nothing and stood awkwardly near each other, the only noise coming from the clanking rim. Frank usually comes to practice tired, having spent all day entertaining Adrian's sister via bootleg DVDs and stolen Candygrams ("Nothing ever happens," he complains, his voice heavy with disappointment). But that night Frank stands with his arms folded across his chest, looking like a satisfied coach.

"I'm a genius," he says.

"We're going to get killed," I say.

"Oh, yeah. That's a fact. But at least we'll be out there."

Adrian's too shy for most conversation.

He's resistant to Frank's wet-fart jokes or my flailing attempts at Klingon. White Mike admires Adrian's closeness to the "majesty of silence." He says there are monks in Tibetan villages who don't come close. The most we get out of Adrian is a grunt/snort thing when he zooms up the court to chase a rebound or corral a loose ball.

"What's your problem?" Frank asked him the other night, his hands curling in pseudo sign language. "Say something."

Adrian shrugged. Often, when we're done playing, he'll sit at half-court and use his fingers to trace strange shapes in the dirt that none of us can make out. Muskrats perched on the pyramids? Dinosaurs entering a pharmacy? Seven-eyed bison? It's the work of a kid who dreams in a different dimension. But that night he wiped some sweat off his forehead with his finger and drew stick figures in the dust. It was so simple, it took me a second to recognize myself. But there I was, standing a head above everybody else, not the ostrich-necked caricature I usually think I look like, but a simple mass of arms, legs, neck, head. It was almost elegant. I didn't notice I was smiling until I saw Adrian smiling back at me.

"My biceps," Frank interrupted. "Make them bigger."

And what about White Mike? He comes to the court in a hoodie and sunglasses. He can't really dribble or shoot or pass, and he jogs in a heavy-shouldered rumble up and down the court.

"I know where my strengths lie," he said once, after Frank begged him to shoot a wide-open lay-up. He passed the ball to me, and I made a bank shot from the free-throw line.

It's become an unspoken rule to discuss his past with a certain delicacy.

"Funny how we're all kinda friends now," I offer tonight.

"Funny, indeed," Mike says.

"Never would've thought I'd be hanging out with a kid like you."

"A kid like me?"

"Who was, like, on TV and stuff."

"What's past is past. I think that's a good thing. Everyone you meet has had multiple lives, multiple versions of themselves in this one life."

And so I stay up tonight thinking about all of us, the misfits and outcasts, our hair cut weirdly and our arms praying-mantis long, our secret pleasures too dorky, our gifts too embarrassing, our pasts too painful, waiting for a chance to find one another.

Even Janae, in her own way, has started to come around. She's our best player. Frank won't admit it, probably because he didn't pick her (the fact that she's a girl might have something to do with it, too), but the rest of us know it. It's hard to describe, but watching her is like watching a great dancer or listening to a great singer or watching a dolphin jumping out of water. It's watching someone do something they've been designed to do. Her shot is automatic, relaxed, and smooth. Her wrist barely flicks, all the movements so connected, it's hard to distinguish one part from the next. Frank watches her jealously, but I like to stand at hovering distance while she warms up.

"Hi," I say as she takes practice shots from three.

She flicks her wrist, and the ball travels in a soft arc, hitting the front of the rim. She steps back and goes through her motion again, trying to figure out what went wrong. Little beads of sweat gather at the edge of her forehead.

"Stop staring," she says.

"Sorry," I mumble.

Tonight I'm standing closer to Janae than I ever have before. We're playing two-on-two, and it's my turn to guard her.

"Get closer," Frank says when I guard her. She's a bucket away from winning.

"I'm already close," I say.

"Closer."

Because we're almost the same height, my chest hovers close to hers. It doesn't seem right to have my hands swarming around her body, so I keep them close to my sides. To my surprise, she doesn't smell like anything at all. When she gives a head fake, my mouth brushes against her cheek.

I step back and put my hands up like I've been caught in the middle of a crime. "Sorry," I say. "Sorry."

But as soon as I step back, she puts the shot up, and before it's even halfway to the rim, she calls game.

CHAPTER 13
HERE GOES NOTHING

The boys from Ghosttown show up in a purple minivan. I expected something different, a luxury bus maybe. A private jet. Something shocking or intimidating. There's something about the minivan that reduces their terror factor a ton.

There's a crowd gathering now. A few people bring blankets so they can watch the slaughter from the grass. Ms. Mayfair is here, and so is Ray the Barber, taking bets on the side. Similac and the rest of the boys park themselves under one of the baskets.

They look at us with these satisfied smiles, like we're on the way to the electric chair.

All the guys from Ghosttown wear arm sleeves and headbands. Some of them still have the tags on their shoes. They stretch nonchalantly with tearaway Windbreakers half-open. They don't even warm up seriously. Instead of shooting lay-ups or jumpers, they chuck the ball one-handed from half-court or shoot the ball backward from the sideline. One of their players does 360 dunks so easily, it looks like he's not even trying. He jumps so high, it looks like he might need a parachute.

Instead of warming up, Frank watches them from half-court.

"They're going to kill us," he says.

"Yeah," I say. "It's been nice knowing you."

There's an old guy with them who stands off to the side, crossing his arms over his chest and looking admiringly at the team. I'm guessing he's their coach. He calls me over.

"Are you playing?" he asks. "Where's the rest of your team?"

"Right there," I say.

He stares at White Mike, who's sitting cross-legged under the basket, trying to control his breathing.

"Him?" the guy says.

"Yeah," I say.

He nods. "Let's make this quick."

Janae shoots for takeout and makes it. Because I'm tall, they put a massive guy on me, this giant scowling kid who's got about six inches on me, easy. That's their first mistake. If they'd been watching warm-ups, they'd know to put someone long on Janae. Instead, they put some little guy on Janae, a kid she can shoot over easily. Frank passes the ball to me and runs off to a corner. White Mike sets a screen for Janae. When she gets the ball at the top of the key, it's up before her man can even get a hand up. Three–nothing.

"Lucky," the guy says.

Janae doesn't even look at him as she jogs back on defense.

Here's how their offense works: Each guy takes a turn being the main guy, and it's not long before they each reveal their tics. The guy I'm guarding likes to do a jump hook over his left shoulder. He's definitely in high school but already has the shadow of a recently shaved beard on his face and neck. I stand tall, with my arms up and my chest out. As he backs into me, I lower my center of gravity so that I won't get pushed back. Still, he scores on me three straight times with the same jump hook. On the fourth try, I try to block it, but I jump right past him. He goes up and under and dunks, sending Mike sprawling into the crowd.

Everyone watching loses their mind. Mike turns red and pounds his fist against a pole.

Adrian brings the ball up the court. The guy that's guarding him has long arms and legs, and from where I'm standing on the baseline, Adrian looks completely engulfed. He spins right and spins left, and the guy stays glued to him. He dribbles toward the middle of the key and looks like he's going to shoot. When two guys bear down on him, he throws me a no-look pass.

I catch the ball. *I catch the ball.* At the beginning of the summer I couldn't even do that. In a panic, I look up to find the center of the backboard and throw the ball up. It misses and clangs off the backboard, but Mike's there to grab the rebound. He throws it to Janae, who flicks her wrist. The net splashes.

What we've learned over the past few days is that none of us except Janae are good enough to beat anybody one-on-one. Adrian's got a nice handle, but his jumper's inconsistent. Mike's no good unless he's two feet from the basket. Frank's pretty good when he's wide open, but if anyone gets close to him, he gets the yips. Me, it's pretty obvious what usually happens when I shoot.

So it's a surprise to everybody that we keep the score close. It's eighteen–thirteen, their lead. Nobody expected this. Especially me.

On defense, the guy I'm guarding gets the ball right on the block. He gives me his up-and-under move, but I stay down. And when he tries to toss a hook shot over me, I'm right there to block it.

Our spectators go silent; I can hear someone opening a bag of chips in the back of the crowd somewhere. I can imagine the looks on everybody's faces. The slack jaws, the surprised eyes. Similac, Ray the Barber, all the kids who wouldn't play with us: They don't even recognize me. Even the kids from Ghosttown scratch the back of their necks. Who knows what'll happen with the rest of the game. With enough luck, we might win. But even if we don't, I know that something's changed. Nobody's going to see me as the kid I was a few weeks ago. Not Mom, not Pop, not Mr. Hunter, not Frank, not Omar, not Janae. Imagine everyone you've ever known not knowing who you really are.

One day they'll ask, *Who are you?*

I don't know, I'll say. *Give me some time, a summer or two to figure it out. See what I become then.*